BEHIND THE SCENES OF

THE INDIAN IN THE CUPBOARD

Adapted by Joan Yankowitz
From the movie *The Indian in the Cupboard*
Screenplay by Melissa Mathison based on the novel by Lynne Reid Banks

SCHOLASTIC INC.

New York Toronto London Auckland Sydney

ISBN 0-590-50984-5

Copyright © 1995 by Paramount Pictures.
All rights reserved. Published by Scholastic Inc.
Adapted from the movie *The Indian in the Cupboard*, screenplay by Melissa Mathison,
based upon the novel by Lynne Reid Banks.

12 11 10 9 8 7 6 5 4 3 2 1   5 6 7 8 9/9 0/0

Printed in the U.S.A   09

First Scholastic printing, July 1995

Omri with the plastic Indian figure he receives for his birthday

Opening

How would you feel if you got a small plastic Indian figure for your birthday and you found out that you could make him come alive? But when he came to life he was still only three inches tall?

Would you tell your parents, your brothers, or your best friend?
Would you hide him in your bedroom?
Would you take him to school?
Would you want to learn about his culture and rituals?
Would you try to find him other friends?

If you answered yes to any of these questions, then you're a lot like Omri, the main character of the movie *The Indian in the Cupboard.*

Ever since a movie producer named Jane Startz read Lynne Reid Banks' exciting book *The Indian in the Cupboard,* she dreamed of bringing the magical story to the movie screen. Ms. Startz said the book showed her "the power of friendship. I wanted to give people the ability to step inside someone else's shoes."

*Producer Jane Startz,
screenwriter Melissa Mathison,
producer Kathleen Kennedy*

It wasn't that easy. Most movies are pretty simple to film. *The Indian in the Cupboard* was much harder to make. After all, two of the main characters, Little Bear (the Indian) and Boone (the Cowboy) were only three inches tall.

The other characters in the movie were all normal-sized. The problem was, how would they put all of them in the film together and still make it look real?
This is the behind-the-scenes story of the making of *The Indian in the Cupboard.*

You'll find out all about the actors, how the kids went to school on the set, what a blue screen is, the secret of oversized props, how they put it all together to make a movie, and much more.

The Screenplay and Screenwriter

Writing a screenplay is the first step in making any movie. A screenplay is simply a play that is written for the screen. Sometimes a screenplay is written from an idea. Other times a screenplay is based on a book. *The Indian in the Cupboard* screenplay is based on a much-loved book that was written by Lynne Reid Banks.

A person who writes a screenplay is called a screenwriter. Melissa Mathison was the screenwriter for *The Indian in the Cupboard.* Ms. Mathison also wrote the screenplays for *E.T. The Extra-Terrestrial* and *The Black Stallion.*

A screenplay or script gives several kinds of information. It shows the words each character will say. These words are called dialogue. The screenplay then tells what the characters do in the scene. Do they sit or stand? Walk, run, enter, or leave a room? Finally the script explains what the movie audience will see up on the screen. Is the camera close to the actors or far away? The script also gives the location of each scene, and tells whether the scene is indoors or outside and what time of day it is. Even with all of these details the screenplay for *The Indian in the Cupboard* was only about 130 pages long!

Director Frank Oz on the set with actor Hal Scardino

Producers

Producers are the people who come up with the idea for a film. Sometimes there is more than one producer on a movie. *The Indian in the Cupboard* had three producers: Jane Startz, Kathleen Kennedy, and Frank Marshall.

Producers have many jobs on a film. They must select the director, figure out how much the movie will cost, and hire the actors.

Executive Producers

Filming a movie is a team effort. The making of *The Indian in the Cupboard* wouldn't have gone as smoothly without the many skills of the executive producers Marty Keltz, Bernie Williams, and Robert A. Harris.

The Director

The director is one of the most important people on a film. A director is the person who takes the screenplay and makes it into a movie. The director picks a crew of camera and other professional people, rehearses the actors, and decides what the camera will shoot.

Frank Oz, the director of *The Indian in the Cupboard,* has had a lot of experience directing major films. Among his movies are *Housesitter, What About Bob?, Dirty Rotten Scoundrels, Little Shop of Horrors,* and *The Dark Crystal.*

Mr. Oz was thrilled to direct the movie. "It was Melissa's beautiful script that drew me in and made me want to be involved with the project," says Mr. Oz.

Before Mr. Oz began to shoot the movie, he needed to know exactly how the action scenes would look when they were filmed. Action scenes are very complicated to film and take a lot of planning. To make sure those scenes turned out the way he wanted, Mr. Oz hired artists to draw the scenes ahead of time. This process is called storyboarding.

For each action scene, Mr. Oz sat down with an artist and told him how he thought the scene should look. He described how the camera would move and at what angles he wanted to shoot.

The artist took this information and drew storyboards, which are sketches that show the scene. Storyboards look like pages from a black-and-white comic book. Sometimes the artist draws five or six storyboards for just one camera shot. An entire action scene can take hundreds of storyboards to lay out.

The Indian in the Cupboard needed storyboards for many scenes because of all the special effects and action scenes. Marc Baird drew many of the storyboards for the movie. "I was hired before the movie began," says Marc. "I read the script, then met with Mr. Oz to talk about specific scenes. He would tell me how he wanted each scene to look, and I would draw the storyboards to show all of the camera moves and angles. It was really a lot of fun."

Most storyboards are finished before the movie begins, but sometimes revisions are made during filming. If Mr. Oz found a better, less expensive way to film a scene, he would ask an artist to draw new storyboards for that scene.

Storyboards weren't done for every scene in *The Indian in the Cupboard*. Many scenes only showed people talking and didn't need to be drawn beforehand. It's a good thing that the movie wasn't *only* made up of action scenes. If it was, artists would have had to draw *many thousands* of storyboards. That's a lot of comic books!

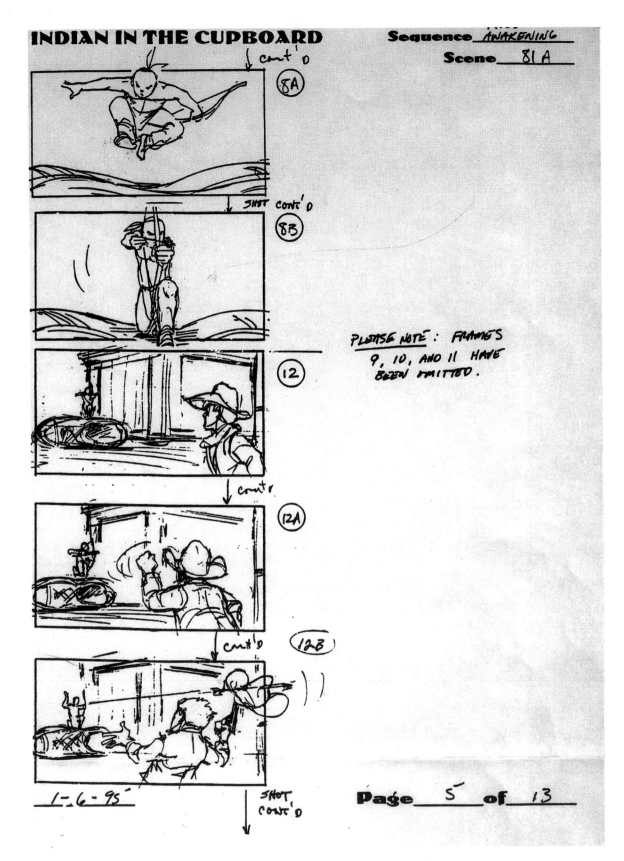

PLEASE NOTE: FRAMES 9, 10, AND 11 HAVE BEEN OMITTED.

1-6-95

Page 5 of 13

Storyboards help the director to plan each shot.

Sketches for the costumes worn by Little Bear, Boone, and Tommy

Director of Photography

The director of photography is the person who takes the movie director's ideas and brings them to life on the screen. The director of photography is in charge of shooting the movie. Russell Carpenter was the director of photography for *The Indian in the Cupboard*. He and Mr. Oz spent many hours discussing which camera angles to use for each scene, where to put the camera for each shot, and what kind of lighting was needed.

The Costume Designer

The costume designer must make sure that all of the characters' clothes look right. Costume designer Deborah Scott had the added job of making sure that the costume she designed for Little Bear was authentic to his culture and his time period. Boone's cowboy costume was also thoroughly researched.

Inside the wardrobe trailer

The Editor

Once the director has finished shooting the film, the editor takes over. The editor must take the thousands of feet of film that have been shot and put it together to make a movie.

The editor is a very important part of the filmmaking process. Ian Crafford was chosen as the editor who would take all of those pieces and make one movie from it. It wasn't an easy task! During filming, the director often shoots the same scene over and over again in order to get a perfect take. Mr. Crafford worked with Mr. Oz to choose the best shots for each of the scenes of the movie.

Then he uses an editing machine, called a moviola, to splice, or join, the film together to make one long movie. You can imagine how complicated that task was with all the special effects in this movie!

Hal Scardino plays Omri.

The Stars

After a casting search in more than 20 cities with over 500 auditions, 10-year-old Hal Scardino was chosen to star as Omri, the lead character. This was Hal's second film. His first role was in the movie *Searching for Bobby Fischer.* Hal was born in Savannah, Georgia, raised in New York City, and now lives in London, England.

Hal loved the excitement of making *The Indian in the Cupboard.* He read the entire script before they even began shooting. Then each day he would go over his lines for the scene they were filming that day. It only took him a couple of minutes every day to learn them, and he didn't forget them when he was on camera.

"The hardest part of acting in the movie was doing scenes over and over again," says Hal. "We did some of them eight or nine times." Every movement had to be exact so that the special effects people could match up the scenes later.

Hal had a full schedule on the set. He explains, "I got up at six forty-five each morning and started shooting at about eight-thirty A.M. I finished up at about five P.M. Then I went to gymnastics or fencing."

In his spare time, Hal managed to stop one of the film crew members from smoking. The crew member had to give Hal a dollar every time he caught her smoking. In two weeks, they were up to 20 dollars. Then Hal gave her the money back. She was so surprised that she quit smoking. And whenever she craved a cigarette, she called Hal for support!

Litefoot plays Little Bear.

Litefoot plays Little Bear, the Onondaga Indian Omri brings to life. The first Native American rap artist and a member of the Cherokee nation, Litefoot has given concerts at Native American reservations and schools for the past two years. This was his first acting role, and he really enjoyed it.

"The way it was made was so interesting," Litefoot says. "Because of how it was filmed, my character never worked directly with Omri. I had to make myself believe that I was really only three inches high, and try to figure out how I would feel being that little. I had to put myself in that world. There were times when Omri shut the cupboard and Little Bear was blown off his feet. That would sure scare someone three inches tall."

During filming, Litefoot was curious about how the movie would look when it was finished. When he saw the final film, it looked so real, Litefoot believed that he actually *was* in the cupboard.

As a Native American, Litefoot was proud to be in this movie because it meant that people would see that there are different tribes all throughout this country and Canada. People would also realize that each of those tribes has its own customs, culture, and traditions. "The movie also teaches us that we can all learn from each other," he says. "Little Bear teaches Omri, and Boone and Little Bear share many experiences."

Litefoot had fun on the set, too. In one scene, Little Bear comes from behind the toy chest and shoots an arrow at Boone. While filming, Litefoot shot the arrow and hit the camera lens—dead on. The arrow cracked the lens! You can bet they had to do *that* take over again!

Rishi Bhat plays Omri's best friend, Patrick.

One day, Rishi Bhat, who plays Patrick, Omri's best friend, received a letter in the mail. It asked, "Does your child want to be an actor?" Rishi asked his dad about it and he was told it was junk mail. Another letter came again the next month and Rishi told his father that he wanted to answer it. His dad told him that he could, but not to count on anything happening. Rishi answered the letter and was called for a screen test. He started to get jobs from that screen test and his acting career had begun.

Ten-year-old Rishi lives in Chicago. Before *The Indian in the Cupboard,* he was in a local stage production and also appeared on the ABC series *Missing Persons.*

Even though Rishi didn't have very much acting experience, he didn't get nervous during shooting. "I didn't have trouble learning my lines," he says.

Rishi had fun working with Omri's on-screen brother Gillon's pet rat. "They only had one rat on the set," he explains. "They used a fake rat during rehearsals because they didn't want to make the rat work so much. Hal was really terrified of the rat. Once, I took the fake rat and put it on his shoulder. He really got scared."

Rishi has had a computer since he was three years old and is a computer whiz. In fact, he helped everyone on the set when they had problems with their computers!

David Keith plays Boone.

David Keith plays Boone, the cowboy who gallops out of the cupboard on his horse. David has a lot of movie experience. His films include *Major League II, An Officer and a Gentleman,* and *Heartbreak Hotel.* He has also appeared in many television miniseries.

Boone, like Little Bear, is only three inches tall, so David was filmed on many oversized sets. His scenes were very complicated. They took hours to rehearse and many takes to film.

The Supporting Cast

The other members of the cast of *The Indian in the Cupboard* all have a lot of film and television experience.

Adiel, Omri's brother, is played by Ryan Olson. Ryan's first movie was *My Girl 2.* He has also appeared in many television shows, including *Cheers* and Disney's *These Friends of Mine.*

Vincent Kartheiser plays Omri's other brother, Gillon. Vincent was recently featured in the lead role of the movie *Heaven Sent.* He also acted in *Little Big League, Iron Will,* and *Untamed Heart.*

Omri's mother, Jane, is played by Lindsay Crouse, an actress who received an Academy Award nomination as Best Supporting Actress for the movie *Places in the Heart.* Ms. Crouse has appeared in many movies and television shows, and has also acted on the Broadway stage.

Richard Jenkins (Omri's father, Vincent) is also a seasoned actor. His films include *Wolf, Undercover Blues,* and *Stealing Home.* He has appeared in many television miniseries.

Rishi Bhat and Hal Scardino on the set

Hal and Rishi's Typical Day

Hal and Rishi spent nine and a half hours a day on *The Indian in the Cupboard* set. They worked for five hours, went to school for three hours, had one hour of rest and recreation, and a half hour for lunch.

Even though they were acting in a movie, Hal and Rishi still had to go to school like any other kids. As you can imagine, their days were really full! Judy Brown was their teacher during filming. She also taught the kids on *Jurassic Park, The Flintstones,* and *The Little Rascals.* "During the filming of *The Indian in the Cupboard,* we always had three hours of school," said Ms. Brown. "When we had a day that wasn't too busy for the kids, we would work longer in school. We would put every extra minute we worked into a 'bank.' Then, for instance, I could tell the production company that Hal had an hour banked. On another day, they would use him an hour more, and school would be an hour shorter."

Hal's real school is in England and Rishi's is in Chicago. At the end of each week, Ms. Brown would send each school all of the work they had done for that week and would get packets of new work for each of them. She kept in close contact with their schools and when the kids were finished filming, they were up-to-date at school.

Both kids took foreign languages. Hal took Latin and French and Rishi took German. A special tutor came in for those lessons.

Hal Scardino and Rishi Bhat work with their teacher.

School was held in a trailer on the set. Ms. Brown taught Rishi, Hal, and Kevin, Hal's photo double. A photo double on a film is a person who is the same size and has the same coloring as one of the actors. A photo double actually takes the place of the actor in the movie when the actor is not available for filming. Hal was only allowed to work on the set for five hours a day, so if filming lasted longer than the five hours, Kevin had to be used as Hal's photo double. In one scene, you think you see Hal's hands. But they are really Kevin's hands, not Hal's!

There was another teacher for the two older boys in the film, Ryan and Vincent. When they filmed the school scenes, all of the children used in those scenes went to school on the set. Their classes were held in the school set that was used in the movie.

Ms. Brown also made sure that the kids got breaks on the set whenever they needed them, and made sure they had rest and recreation.

Hal and Rishi use sign language in the movie. A teacher came to the set just to teach them the sign language they'd need in the film. "It wasn't hard to learn," Rishi says. "It only took a couple of minutes. And it was fun."

The kids loved to play Ping-Pong. In fact, a Ping-Pong table was set up on a soundstage for the whole time they were filming. They even had Ping-Pong tournaments.

Hal Scardino and Rishi Bhat made the volcano used in the movie.

How They Found Artwork to Use in the School Scene

In the movie, there is a classroom scene where the children show projects that they have been working on. The prop department didn't know where to get these projects so they asked Ms. Brown to have Hal and Rishi make them in school.

The kids made a volcano and a relief map out of flour and water. They used beans and peas to show the mountain ranges, rivers, and lakes. Both projects were shown in the movie. Other kids who worked on the movie also made projects that were featured in the film. Did you notice the different projects when you saw the movie?

How They Put It All Together

As you can imagine, it was very difficult and complicated to make *The Indian in the Cupboard.* Before they started shooting, executive producer Bernie Williams said, "How on earth will we put a three-inch character into a scene with normal-sized people?" Mr. Williams said that this was the toughest of his 45 movies to produce. "It was so technical," he says. "Audiences today have higher standards, and they expect us to make it look real."

Giant props, like this baseball, helped make it look as if Boone and Little Bear were only three inches tall.

It took a team of top professionals to make it all work together. Leslie McDonald, the production designer, had to come up with the oversized sets and props that were used in the movie. It was a real challenge for her!

The production design team decided that Little Bear should be small enough to fit in the palm of Omri's hand. From that, they figured out that Little Bear and Boone should be three inches tall, and Omri and the rest of the big characters should be 24 times larger.

"In order to show that Little Bear and Boone were so small, we had to build many gigantic sets and props for them," says Ms. McDonald. "We made about one hundred different oversized props, including a baseball, a tepee, the longhouse, the seed tray that Little Bear lives in, the bedpost, sections of beds, the Lego box that Omri carries Little Bear around in, a fanny pack, a sneaker, part of a garden in the backyard, and trees."

Boone stands on the oversized bedpost. The monitor in the foreground helps the director see what the shot will look like on film.

This crew member is holding the small-sized cupboard that Omri receives for a present.
The oversized set of the cupboard is in the background.

In some scenes, Little Bear stands in front of a wall in Omri's room. Since Little Bear is only supposed to be three inches tall, they had to show that the wall was enormous to him. For those scenes, the production design department built a huge wall and baseboard on one of the soundstages. When you saw the movie, you probably didn't realize that the actual wall was the size of a football field!

More than 70 carpenters and 25 sculptors worked on the set each day. There was a lot to do. They worked hard to make sure that the look and texture of the giant props were realistic. In one case, they even hand-wove the fabric of an immense fanny pack to match the grain of Omri's regular-sized fanny pack. It took hours and hours!

Three different-sized cupboards were used in the movie—a small cupboard, a cupboard 24 times larger than the small cupboard, and an in-between-sized cupboard that was used in the superhero scene. In that scene, all of the superhero characters come alive and start fighting with each other. Could you tell which cupboard was which?

In another scene, Boone is walking around on Omri's bed. They actually filmed him on an oversized prop bed. The blanket on the bed is sculpted exactly to match the scaled-down version of the blanket. Since each blanket was shot on a different piece of film, everything had to match exactly when they put the film all together. If the film hadn't matched, there would have been a gap between Boone's feet and the blanket. Boone would have looked as if he were walking on air in the final movie!

Along with the oversized sets and props, a special effect, blue-screen technique was used in some of the scenes involving Little Bear and Boone. Industrial Light & Magic, the folks who brought you the special effects in movies like *Star Wars* and *Jurassic Park,* were in charge of designing the special visual effects for *The Indian in the Cupboard.*

Little Bear builds the longhouse; the blue screen is behind him. The screen won't show up on the movie film.

What an incredible process! First they filmed a scene's background. Then they went to a special stage with a blue screen, like a movie screen. Using special cameras that filtered out the blue screen, they filmed the actors from far away so they looked very small. All that showed up on the film were the tiny actors.

During post-production, the special effects wizards put the film of the small Little Bear and Boone on top of the film of the normal-sized background. In the final movie, the characters really look as if they're just three inches tall!

Cast and crew film on the longhouse set. The movie camera was placed far away so that the characters and the set would look small. The oversized wall and baseboard set are in the background. The wall is actually the size of a football field!

It wasn't easy to find a soundstage big enough to film some scenes. Because a normal-sized person is 24 times bigger than Little Bear and Boone, the camera sometimes had to be moved back 100 feet and moved up in the air 100 feet to shoot the tiny characters in front of the blue screen. They almost ran out of room!

Somehow it all worked. "It was important to us that the action in the movie seem as normal as possible," says Eric Brevig, Industrial Light & Magic supervisor. "Because of that, we had to develop new special effects techniques especially for this movie.

"In *Jurassic Park*, we had to combine animated dinosaurs with live actors," Eric says. "We thought that was hard. But filming *The Indian in the Cupboard* was even more difficult. We had to combine live miniature actors and horses with live regular-sized people and backgrounds."

It wasn't easy. To make those scenes look real, the special effects people first used traditional motion control photography to film the background. That means they didn't have a person behind the camera. They used computers to program the cameras ahead of time and the computers controlled the actual filming.

Then they filmed the actors, using state-of-the-art advanced computer graphics techniques. That was where they filmed the actors in front of the blue screen. Even though they used similar techniques in *Jurassic Park*, they still had to invent new techniques for *The Indian in the Cupboard* because they were filming live actors, not animated dinosaurs.

Boone works on the longhouse set. A technician holds a boom microphone to help catch every line of Boone's dialogue.

"It was the first time we've ever tried to put these two camera techniques together using live people," says Eric. "It set new standards for the industry." One scene was particularly hard to film. In the scene, Patrick brings Boone to life in the cupboard. Boone comes out on his horse. The horse gets scared and gallops the length of the table that the cupboard is on. When they get to the end of the table, the horse stops short, but Boone keeps going and falls onto Omri's bed.

Remember that Boone and his horse are only supposed to be three inches tall! To get the proper camera perspective for the scene, the filmmakers built a wooden platform on top of a soundstage and put a blue screen against the wall above the platform. Then, from a far distance, they filmed a stuntman galloping on a horse along the platform. At a specific point, the horse was told to stop short.

The stuntman was wearing a special wire that pulled him into the air so he looked as if he were thrown from the horse. Even though it was a complicated shot, it worked perfectly. Actually, it was probably fun for everyone but the stuntman!

Boone and Little Bear were almost always filmed on the oversized sets or in front of the blue screen. The only time they weren't was during the movie's dream sequence, where all the characters are the same size. In that scene, everyone was filmed in regular size.

It would have been impossible to build entire rooms on an oversized scale. They would have taken up too much space. For scenes that took place in a large portion of a room, the actors were made smaller by using the blue screen technique. If the scene involved only a small part of the room, it was more economical to build an oversized set or prop.

Hal Scardino was on location in New York City for this shot.

The Shooting Schedule

The Indian in the Cupboard was filmed mainly on five soundstages in Culver City, California. But, because it was important to establish that the movie takes place in New York City, the outside scenes were all filmed on the Lower East Side of New York City.

The actors and crew went on location to New York for a few weeks, where they filmed the exteriors of Omri's house, school, the hardware store that he goes to, and the street scenes going to and from his school.

The production designers spent a lot of time researching the type of house that Omri might live in, and how it would be furnished. They also wanted to know what his school would have looked like, and what kinds of classrooms were in the school. Then they designed the interiors on a soundstage in California.

Director Frank Oz works with Hal Scardino on the full-sized set of Omri's bedroom. Notice the radiator in the background.

Director Frank Oz works with Litefoot on the oversized set of the lower part of the radiator.

The interiors were filmed on a soundstage because it gave the filmmakers more control over lighting and they didn't have to worry about bad weather.

Some of the school hallway and classroom scenes were shot at a school in Los Angeles. It took four days to complete this location shooting. A school set was built on a soundstage to film the other classroom scenes in which Omri is reading his journal.

The Indian in the Cupboard took four months to film, with an extra month added just for shooting blue screen scenes.

The daily shooting schedule was very demanding. There are very strict laws regulating how many hours a child actor can work in a day. So any scenes that the kids were in were finished by 5:00 P.M. The crew moved over to the oversized stage at about 6:00 P.M. and finished shooting the scenes with adults at 8:30 P.M. In the morning the cast rehearsed scenes that would be shot in front of the blue screen and the crew prepared the camera angles. Those scenes were shot between 3:00 and 5:00 P.M. every day. Whew!

"THE INDIAN IN THE CUPBOARD"

FEATURE CALL SHEET

Production Number 33025	W.A. No. IC1455	Date: **THURSDAY JANUARY 26, 1995**
		(day / date / mo.yr.)
Producer(s): K. Kennedy, F. Marshall, B. Williams		Day **77** of **84** Days
Director: Frank Oz		Crew Call: 7:30 AM · Shooting Call: 8:15 AM
Sunrise:	Weather:	Cast Rehearsal:
Sunset:		

NOTE: THERE WILL BE NO FORCED CALLS WITHOUT PRIOR APPROVAL BY UPM (no exceptions).....ALL CALLS SUBJECT TO CHANGE BY U.P.M. - AND/OR A.D.'S.....NO PERSONAL VIDEO CAMERAS ALLOWED OR USED ON SET.

SCHEDULE

SET DESCRIPTION	SCENES	CAST #'S	D/N	PAGES	LOCATION
INT - Omri's Bedroom	119Apt.	1, 3	Night 4	tbd	Stage 25
(Omri & Patrick push the bed away.)					Sony Studios
INT - Omri's Bedroom	28pt.	1	Night 2	tbd	
(Omri reacts to Super Heroes.)					
INT - OS Pillow / Seed Tray	120Bpt., 121pt.	2, 8, 15	Night 4	tbd	Stage 27
(Tommy fixes Boone...Boone wakes.)	(OS Shot #TBD)				
INT - OS Cupboard	119Bpt.	15	Night 4	tbd	Stage 25
(Tommy comes back.)	(OS Shot #27B, 30, 32-32A)				
INT - OS Cupboard	121pt.	15	Night 4	tbd	
(Tommy leaves again.)	(OS Shot #1-1A)				
~ REHEARSE & PRE-LIGHT ~					
INT - OS Full Cupboard	28pt.	Super Heroes	Night 2	tbd	Stage 27
(Super Hero Figures come alive.)					

~ BLUESCREEN UNIT (per Bluescreen Call Sheet) ~

TALENT

K = Minors under 18

#	CAST & DAY PLAYERS	ROLE	PU/LEAVE	MAKEUP	SET CALL	REMARKS
1	Hal Scardino (K9)	Omri	~	7:30 AM	8:15 AM	self-drive
2	Litefoot	Little Bear	8:15 AM	8:45 AM	W/N	p/up @ Marina Point
3	Rishi Bhat (K10)	Patrick	~	7:30 AM	8:15 AM	self-drive
8	David Keith	Boone	7:30 AM	8:00 AM	9:00 AM	p/up @ home
15	Steve Coogan	Tommy	9:30 AM	9:45 AM	11:00 AM	p/up @ Loew's S. M.
	J.R. Horsting	Robocop	~	~	5:00 PM	
	Tom Bewley	Darth Vader	Travel to Los Angeles			
	Keii Johnston	GI Joe	~	~	5:00 PM	
	Michael Papajohn	Cardassian	~	~	5:00 PM	
	Eric Stabenau	Ferengi	~	~	5:00 PM	
	Dennis Scott	Stunt Coordinator	~	~	5:00 PM	

* N.D. Breakfast

ATMOSPHERE AND STANDINS

ATMOSPHERE AND STANDINS		SPECIAL INSTRUCTIONS
1 stand-in ("Omri")	rpt. to stage 25 @ 7:30 am	• NO SMOKING ON STAGE.
1 stand-in ("Patrick")	rpt. to stage 25 @ 7:30 am	• SAFETY IS EVERYONE'S CONCERN. PLEASE NOTIFY AN
1 stand-in ("Little Bear")	rpt. to stage 27 @ 9 am	A.D. OF ANY SAFETY HAZARD YOU ENCOUNTER!
1 stand-in ("Boone")	rpt. to stage 27 @ 9 am	• PLEASE DO NOT DISTURB PROPS OR SET DRESSING.
1 stand-in ("Tommy")	rpt. to stage 27 @ 9 am	
5 stand-ins ("Super Heroes")	rpt. to stage 27 @ 3 pm	
		• Dailies @ wrap - Tri-Star Building - Rm. #24.

ADVANCE SHOOTING NOTES

Date	Scene #'s	Set Description/Location	Cast	D/N	Pages
Day 78	28pt.	INT - OS Full Cupboard - Stage 27	Super Heroes	Night 2	tbd
Friday 1/27/95	72Bpt., 72Cpt.	INT - OS Radiator - Stage 27	2	Day 3	tbd
	119Apt.	INT - OS Floor / Crack - Stage 27	2	Night 4	tbd
	119Bpt. if not complete	INT - OS Cupboard - Stage 25	15	Night 4	tbd
	121pt. if not complete	INT - OS Cupboard - Stage 25	15	Night 4	tbd
	BLUE SCREEN UNIT - PER BLUESCREEN CALL SHEET				
Day 79 Monday 1/30/95		TBD			

UPM	Bernie Williams	First Asst. Dir.:	Michele Panelli-Venetis
Prod. Ofc. Phone:	(310) 280-8882	2nd Asst. Dir.:	David Fudge, Stephen Hagen (818) 347-2229

The call sheet tells what scenes will be shot each day, which cast and crew members will be needed for the shots, and what time each cast and crew member must report to the set.

"THE INDIAN IN THE CUPBOARD"

FEATURE CALL SHEET

Date: THURS. JAN. 26, 1995

	NO	STAFF AND CREW (Crew names to be inserted)		TIME		NO	STAFF AND CREW (Crew names to be inserted)		TIME	NO	STAFF AND CREW (Crew names to be inserted)		TIME
PRODUCTION	1	UPM	Bernie Williams	O/C	MAKEUP/HAIR	1	Key Make-Up	F. Bowring	6:42 a		CATERING		
	1	Prod. Supv.	M. Wright	O/C		1	Make-Up	K. Fry	6:42 a		Caterer		
	1	1st Asst. Dir.	M. Venetis	7:30 a		1	Key Hairstylist	L. Waggoner	6:42 a		Cook's Helper		
	1	2nd Asst. Dir.	D. Fudge	7:12 a		1	Hairstylist	L. Meyers	6:42 a		Breakfast Ready at		
	1	2nd 2nd A.D.	S. Hagen	6:42 a			Add'l. M/Up				Lunches Ready at		
		Add'l. 2nd A.D.					Add'l. Hair				2nd Meal Ready at		
	1	Set Asst.	B. Manis	7:12 a	PROPS	1	Propmaster	R. Miller	7:30 a		MISC. PERSONNEL		
	1	Set Asst.	S. Mathison	7:12 a		1	Asst. Props.	T. Altobello	7:30 a	1	Teacher	J. Brown	7:30 a
	1	P.O.C.	D. Williams	O/C		1	Asst. Props.	Stubblefield	7:30 a		Add'l. Teach.		
	1	Asst. P.O.C.	J. Fishman	O/C						1	Cast Guardian	W. Noonan	7:30 a
	1	Office Asst.	Glickman	O/C	SP. EFX	1	Sp. Efx. Coord.	M. Lanteri	O/C	1	Publicist	A. Reilly	O/C
	1	Office Asst.	Schwartz	O/C		1	Sp. Efx. Supv.	D. Blitstein	O/C	1	Reader	M. Warwick	10:30 a
	1	Asst. to Dir.	L. Converse	O/C		1	Sp. Efx.	G. Tippie	7:30 a		Dialogue Coach		
	1	Asst. to Prod.	C. Dahm	O/C							RIGGING ELECTRIC & GRIP		
	1	Prod. Acct.	T. Pearson	O/C						1	Rigging Gaffer	D. Kerns	O/C
	1	Asst. Acct.	D. Tieman	O/C						1	Electrical	McMillan	O/C
	1	Const. Acct.	R. Steele	O/C	ART DEPT.	1	Prod. Designer	L. McDonald	O/C	2	Electrical	Koski/Tomich	O/C
	1	Payroll Asst.	C. Pike	O/C		1	Art Director	T. Fanning	O/C	1	Rigg. Key Grip	D. Hennes	O/C
	1	Acct. Asst.	L. Roberts	O/C			Asst. Art Dir.			1	Grip	Nieuwenhuis	O/C
	1	Acct. PA	S. Boyd	O/C		1	Art Dept Coord	Richardson	O/C	1	Grip	Montesanto	O/C
	1	Script Supv.	L. Kouimelis	7:30 a			Set Designer			1	Grip	T. Johnson	O/C
SET OPS.		First Aid	(per studio hospital)				Set Designer				Grip		
		Fire Safety Officer(Studio)		per dept.		1	Set Designer	B. A. Jaeckel	O/C		Grip		
		Studio Guards		per dept.			Set Designer				INDUSTRIAL LIGHT & MAGIC		
	1	Craft Service	J.J. Geary	6:30 a		1	Storyboards	M. Baird	O/C	1	Vis. Efx. Supv.	E. Brevig	O/C
		Add'l. CSE				1	Comp. Modeler	T. Clark	O/C	1	Vis. Efx. Prod.	C. England	O/C
LOCATION		Location Mgr.				1	Art Dept Asst.	Von Seeburg	O/C	1	Vis. Efx. Coord.	E. Wangberg	O/C
		Asst. Loc. Mgr.		per dept.			Art Dept PA				EQUIPMENT		
		Police Officers			CONSTRUCTION	1	Const. Coord.	J. Passanante	O/C	X	Camera Pkg.(s)		
		Fire Safety				1	Const. Foreman	J. Davis	O/C	X	Sound Pkg.		
		Security (Loc.)		↓		1	Const. Foreman	P. Lamppu	O/C	X	Video Pkg.		
CAMERA	1	Dir. Photo.	R. Carpenter	7:30 a		1	Paint Supv.	T. Brown	O/C	27	Walkie Talkies		
	1	Cam. Opr.	B. Roe	7:30 a		1	Paint Foreman	G. Osborn	O/C	16	Head Sets/Handmikes		
		Add'l. Opr.				1	S/By Painter	T. Ackers	7:30 a		Air Conditioner(s)		
	1	1st A.C.	R. Morey	7:12 a		1	Labor Foreman	A. Saso	O/C	1	Portable Dressing Room		
		Add'l. 1st				1	Mill Foreman	C. Cetrone	O/C		Dressing Rm. (Heidelberg)		
	1	2nd A.C.	T. Gombart	7:12 a		1	S/By Const.	P. Lamppu	7:30 a	1	Recreation Trailer		
		Hot Head Tech				1	Set Decorator	C. Spellman	O/C		VEHICLES/EQUIPMENT		
	1	Loader	A. LaLicata	7:12 a	SET DECORATING	1	Leadperson	S. Bobbitt	O/C		Production Van(s)		per dept.
	1	Wilcam 1st AC	P. Schmitt	O/C			Set Dresser			1	Camera Truck		
	1	Still Photo	Z. Rosenthal	O/C		1	Swing Gang	G. Brewer	O/C	1	Prop Trlr.		
SOUND	1	Mixer	A. Rochester	7:30 a		1	Swing Gang	J. Bedig	O/C	1	Grip/Electric Trlr.		
	1	Boom	R. Johnson	7:30 a		1	Swing Gang	N. Parker	O/C	1	Construction Trlr.		
	1	2nd Boom	J. Wolpa	7:12 a		1	On-Set Dresser	K. Cossette	7:30 a	1	EFX Trlr.		
		Playback				1	On-Set Dresser	L. Corbin	7:30 a	1	CSE Truck		
	1	Video Assist	C. McLean	7:12 a		1	Greens Foreman	Butterworth	O/C		Set Dressing - 5T		
GRIP	1	Key Grip	L. Moriarity	7:30 a		1	S/By Greens	H. Herrera	7:30 a	1	Wardrobe Trlr.		
	1	2nd Grip	E. Kerry	7:30 a	TRANSPORTATION	1	Trans. Coord.	G. Veilleux	per dept.	1	Make-Up Trlr.		
	1	Dolly Grip	D. Chartier	7:30 a		1	Trans. Capt.	S. Brodsky			Motorhome(s)		
	1	Grip	J. Johnson	7:30 a		1	Driver	C. Fehrman		5	Crew Cab(s)		
	2	Grip	Wade/Duran	7:30 a		1	Driver	W. McClain			Cube Van(s)		
	2	Grip	Harjo/Whitmore	7:30 a		1	Driver	R. Cafferty			Maxi-Van(s)		
		Grip				1	Driver	D. Wood		4	Mini-Van(s)		
ELECTRIC	1	Chief Light Tech	R. West	7:30 a		1	Driver	P. Moran			Cast Car(s)		
	1	Asst Light Tech	S. Cohagan	7:30 a		1	Driver	J. Drucker			Honeywagon (__ rooms)		
	1	Elect.	R. Gittens	7:30 a		1	Driver	B. Defont		2	Cast Trlr. (single)		
	1	Elect.	R. Gonzales	7:30 a		1	Driver	F. Ingham		3	Cast Trlr. (double)		
	1	Elect.	K. Bonet	7:30 a			Driver			1	School Trlr.		
	1	Elect.	Erickson	7:30 a			Driver				Insert Car		
	1	Elect.	Neal	7:30 a			Driver		↓		Generator		
WARDROBE	1	Costume Dsgnr.	D. Scott	O/C		10	Total Drivers				Crane(s)		
	1	Costume Supv.	M. Grimaud	O/C							Scissor Lift(s)		
	1	Set Costumer	V. Zielonka	7:12 a			Wrangler(s)				Other:		
	1	Set Costumer	A. Martin	7:12 a			Wrangler(s)						
		Costumer					Animal Trainer						
		Ager/Dyer											↓

SPECIAL NOTES: **PROPS:** Seed Tray w/ Long House, Patrick's Sleeping Bag, Cupboard & Key, Flashlight, Chief Toy,
Action Figures, Arrow in Boone, Syringe, Tommy's Medical Bag.

WARDROBE:	Blood & Mud Spattered, Boone Shirt is Bloody.	**SP EFX:**	Retractable Syringe.	
CAMERA:	Wilcam.	**ELECT.:**	High Powered Flashlight.	
VISUAL EFX:	Vistavision (Shot #TBD - Sc. 28pt.)	**MAKE-UP:**	Little Bear's Tattoos, Blood, Tommy's Muddy Hands.	

First Assistant Director:	Second Assistant Director:	Unit Production Manager:
Michele Panelli-Venetis	David Fudge, Stephen Hagen	Bernie Williams

FORM NO. PF 920 a back (Rev. 6/94)

"THE INDIAN IN THE CUPBOARD"

FEATURE DAILY PRODUCTION REPORT

Date: **WEDNESDAY, JANUARY 25, 1995**
(day/date/mo./year)

Producer(s): KATHLEEN KENNEDY, FRANK MARSHALL, BERNIE WILLIAMS

Director: FRANK OZ

Day # 76 of 84*

Prod. No. 33025

Weather:

	1ST UNIT	2ND UNIT	REHEARSE	TEST	TRAVEL	UNWORKED HOLIDAYS	TURN-AROUND	RETAKES ADD'D SC	TOTAL
NO. DAYS SCHEDULED	84	~	10	5	1	8	~	X	108
NO. DAYS ACTUAL	76	~	10	6	1	9	~	~	102

STATUS OF SHOOTING

DATE STARTED: 9/15/94
SCHEDULED FINISH: 1/27/95 (main) 2/15/95 (blue)
REVISED FINISH: 2/2/95**

NAME OF SET	LOCATION	SCENE #'S
INT. OS PILLOW/SEED TRAY	STAGE 27	116comp., 119comp. 119Apt 120pt. 120Bpt., 121pt.

[X] ON SCHEDULE
[ ] AHEAD ___ DAYS
[ ] BEHIND ___ DAYS

	SCENES	PAGES		MINUTES	SET-UPS
SCRIPT	133	106			
TAKEN PREV.	102	87	PREV.	1:38:29	831
TAKEN TODAY	2	1 1/8	TODAY	0:01:31	9
TOTAL TO DATE	104	88 1/8	TOTAL	1:40:00	840
TO BE TAKEN	29	17 7/8			

SCENES COMPLETED:
116comp., 119comp., 119Apt.
120pt., 120Bpt., 121pt

SCHED. BUT NOT SHOT:

SC'S/ELEMENTS OMITTED:

SPECIAL NOTES:

CREW CALL: 7:30 A
SHOOTING CALL: 8:45 A
FIRST SHOT: 10:36 A
MEAL OUT: 1:30 P
MEAL IN: 2:30 P
FIRST SHOT: 5:16 P
MEAL OUT: ~
MEAL IN: ~
CAMERA WRAP: 8:15 P
CREW WRAP: 8:15 P
LAST MAN OUT: 11:00 P
LAST ARR. @ HQ.

FILM INVENTORY

STARTING INVENTORY: 424,000
ADDITIONAL REC'D: ~
TOTAL REC'D: 424,000
TOTAL USED: 344,410
BALANCE ON HAND: 79,590

FILM USE	GOOD	NO GOOD	WASTE	TOTAL	1/4" ROLLS
PREVIOUS	171,510	153,629	16,931	342,070	182
TODAY	1,200	1,120	20	2,340	2
TO DATE	172,710	154,749	16,951	344,410	184

CAST - WEEKLY & DAY PLAYERS

WORKED-W STARTED-S TRAVEL-TR	REHEARSAL-R HOLD-H	FINISHED-F TEST-T	W H S F R T TR	M/UP WDBE.	REPORT ON SET	DISMISS ON SET	OUT	IN	LEAVE FOR LOC.	ARRIVE ON LOC.	LEAVE LOC.	ARRIVE AT HDQ.
	CAST		BKFST									
1) OMRI - H. Scardino*		(M)	W	~	8:00A	2:00 P	1:00 P	2:00 P				
2) LITTLE BEAR - Litefoot			X W	5:35 A	9:15 A	8:25 P	1:30 P	2:30 P				
3) PATRICK - Rishi Bhat*		(M)	W	~	8:00A	2:00 P	1:00 P	2:00 P				
8) BOONE - David Keith			W	8:30A	9:15 A	7:30 P	1:30 P	2:30 P				
15) TOMMY - Steve Coogan			W	10:00 A	11:30 A	8:15 P	1:30 P	2:30 P				
XX STUNT COOR - Dennis Scott			H									
XX GI JOE - Keii Johnson**			SH									
XX FERENGI - Eric Stabenau**			SH									
XX CARDASSIAN - Michael Papajohn**			SH									

*= School only (Not photographed)
**= Not photographed
(M) = Minor 1 = 1 MPV @ wrap

INDICATE STUNT ADJUSTMENTS

ALL SAG OUT TIMES INCL. CONTRACTUAL 15 MINUTE CLEANUP

EXTRA TALENT / MUSICIANS, ETC.

NO.	RATE	CALL	DISMISS	MEAL	MPV	ADJ.	NO.	RATE	CALL	DISMISS	MEAL	MPV	ADJ.
1	$90.00	7:30 A	10:00 A	~	~	~							
1	$90.00	7:30 A	8:24 P	1:30-2:30p	~	~							
1	$90.00	10:00 A	8:24 P	1:30-2:30p	~	~							
1	$90.00	9:15 A	8:30 P	1:30-2:30p	~	~							

ASSISTANT DIRECTORS: Michele Panelli-Venetis, David Fudge

UNIT PRODUCTION MANAGER: Bernie Williams

FORM NO PF 405 (5/94)

The daily production report gives a summary of what was accomplished in the previous day's work.

"THE INDIAN IN THE CUPBOARD"

Date: WEDNESDAY, JAN. 25, 1995

#	STAFF AND CREW (Crew names to be inserted)		TIME IN	OUT	#	STAFF AND CREW (Crew names to be inserted)		TIME IN	OUT	#	STAFF AND CREW (Crew names to be inserted)		TIME IN	OUT
PRODUCTION					**MAKEUP/HAIR**									
1	UPM	Bernie Williams	O/C	O/C	1	Make-Up	F. Bowring	5:12a	8:54p		CATERING			
1	Prod. Supv.	M. Wright	O/C	O/C	1	Add'l MU	K. Fry	8:15a	8:54p		Caterer			
1	1st Asst. Dir.	M. Venetis	7:30a	8:15p	1	Hairstylist	L. Waggoner	5:12a	848p		Cook's Helper(s)			
1	2nd Asst. Dir.	D. Fudge	7:12a	8:45p	1	Add'l Hair	L. Meyers	8:15a	848p		Cook's Helper(s)			
1	2nd 2nd A.D.	S. Hagen	5:12a	8:45p		Add'l M/U					Breakfasts			
	2nd 2nd					Add'l Hair					Lunches			
2	Set Asst.	Mathison/Manis	7:12a	8:45p	**PROPS**						2nd Meal Ready at			
1	P.O.C.	D. Williams	O/C	O/C	1	Propmaster	R. Miller	7:30a	8:48p		MISC. PERSONNEL			
1	Asst. P.O.C.	J. Fishman	O/C	O/C	1	Asst. Props.	T. Altobello	7:30a	8:48p	1	Teacher	J. Brown	9:00a	1230p
1	Office Asst.	A. Glickman	O/C	O/C	1	Asst. Props.	Stubblefield	7:30a	7:30p		Add'l Teacher			
1	Office Asst.	Schwartz	O/C	O/C		Asst. Props					Publicist	A. Reilly	O/C	O/C
1	Asst. to Dir.	L. Converse	O/C	O/C	**SP. EFX**						Dialogue Coach		O/C	O/C
1	Asst. to Prod.	C. Dahm	O/C	O/C	1	Sp. Efx. Coord.	M. Lanteri	O/C	O/C		Onandaga Adv			
1	Prod. Acct.	T. Pearson	O/C	O/C	1	Sp. Efx. Supv.	D. Blitstein	O/C	O/C		Lang. Teacher			
1	Asst. Acct.	D. Tiernan	O/C	O/C	1	Efx.	G. Tippie	7:30a	8:24p		RIGGING GRIP/ELECT.			
1	Const. Acct.	R. Steele	O/C	O/C	1	Efx.	D. Peterson	7:30a	8:24p	1	Rigging Gaffer	D. Kerns	O/C	O/C
1	Payroll Asst.	C. Pike	O/C	O/C		Puppet Tech.				1	Elect.	MacMillan	O/C	O/C
1	Acct. Asst.	L. Roberts	O/C	O/C		Puppet Tech.					Gen Op.			
1	Acct. PA	S. Boyd	O/C	O/C	1	Prod. Designer	L. McDonald	O/C	O/C	1	Key Rig Grip	Hennes	O/C	O/C
1	Script Supv.	L. Kouimelis	7:30a	11:00p	1	Art Director	T. Fanning	O/C	O/C	2	Rig Grip	Montesanto/Johnson	O/C	O/C
SET OPS.	First Aid				1	Asst. Art Dir.				1	Rig Grip	Nieuwenhuis	O/C	O/C
	Fire Safety Officer (Studio)				1	Art Dept Coord	Richardson	O/C	O/C		Test Grip			
	Studio Guards					Set Designer					INDUSTRIAL LIGHT & MAGIC			
1	Craft Service	J.J. Geary	6:30a	9:30p		Set Designer				1	Vis. Efx Supv.	E. Brevig	O/C	O/C
	Craft Service				1	Set Designer	B. A. Jaeckel	O/C	O/C	1	Vis. Efx Prod.	C. England	O/C	O/C
LOCATION	Location Mgr.					Set Designer				1	Vis. Efx Coord.	E. Wangberg	O/C	O/C
	Asst. Loc. Mgr.				1	Storyboards	M. Baird	O/C	O/C					
	Police Officers				1	Comp. Modeler	T. Clark	O/C	O/C		EQUIPMENT			
	Fire Safety				1	Art Dept Asst.	Von Seeburg	O/C	O/C	X	Camera Pkg.(s)			
	Security (Loc.)					Art Dept PA				X	Sound Pkg.			
CAMERA					**CONSTRUCTION**					X	Video Pkg.			
1	Dir. Photo.	R. Carpenter	7:30a	8:12p	1	Const. Coord.	J. Passanante	O/C	O/C	27	Walkie Talkies			
1	Cam. Opr.	B. Roe	7:30a	8:24p	1	Const. Foreman	J. Davis	O/C	O/C	19	Head Sets/Handmikes			
	Hot Head Tech				1	Const. Foreman	P. Lamppu	O/C	O/C		Power Pod w/Tech			
1	1st A.C.	R. Morey	7:12a	9:00p	1	Paint Supv.	T. Brown	O/C	O/C	1	Portable Dressing Room			
	Add'l 1st AC				1	Paint Foreman	G. Osborn	O/C	O/C		Dressing Room(s)	Heidlberg		
1	2nd A.C.	T. Gombart	7:12a	9:00p	1	S/By Painter	T. Ackers	7:30a	8:30p		Lenny Arm			
1	Wil Cam 1st AC	P. Schmitt			1	Labor Foreman	A. Saso	O/C	O/C		VEHICLES/EQUIPMENT			
1	Loader	A. Lalicata	7:12a	9:00p	1	Mill Foreman	C. Cetrone	O/C	O/C		Production Van(s)			
	Add'l 2nd AC					S/By Const.				1	Camera Truck			
1	Still Photo	Z. Rosenthal	O/C	O/C	1	Set Decorator	C. Spelman	O/C	O/C	1	Prop Trlr.			
SOUND					1	Leadperson	S. Bobbitt	O/C	O/C	1	Grip/Electric Trlr.			
1	Mixer	A. Rochester	7:30a	8:42p		Set Dresser				1	Construction Trlr.			
1	Boom	R. Johnson	7:30a	8:42p	**SET DECORATING**					1	EFX Trlr.			
1	2nd Boom	J. Wolpa	7:12a	8:42p	1	Swing Gang	G. Brewer	O/C	O/C	1	CSE Truck			
	Playback				1	Swing Gang	J. Bedig	O/C	O/C		Set Dressing - 5T			
1	Video Assist	C. McLean	7:12a	9:18p	1	Swing Gang	N. Parker	O/C	O/C	1	Wardrobe Trlr.			
	Video Assist				1	On-Set Dresser	K. Cossette	7:30a	8:48p	1	Make-Up Trlr.			
GRIP					1	On-Set Dresser	L. Corbin	O/C	O/C	5	Crew Cab(s)			
1	Key Grip	L. Moriarty	7:30a	8:30p	1	Greens Foreman	Ayers	O/C	O/C		Maxi-Van(s)			
1	2nd Grip	E. Kerry	7:30a	8:30p	1	Stby Greens	Herrera	730a	8:48p	4	Mini-Van(s)			
1	Dolly Grip	Chartier	7:30a	8:30p	1	Trans. Coord.	G. Veilleux	O/C	O/C		Cast Car(s)			
1	Grip	Johnson	7:30a	8:30p	1	Trans. Capt.	S. Brodsky	O/C	O/C		Honeywagon (_8_ rooms)			
2	Grip	Duran/Wade	7:30a	8:30p	1	Driver	C. Fehrman	600a	930p	2	Cast Trlr. (single)			
3	Grip Antonetti	Harjo/Whitmore	7:30a	8:30p	1	Driver	W. McClain	430a	700p	4	Cast Trlr. (double)			
ELECTRIC					1	Driver	R. Cafferty	700a		1	School Trlr.			
1	Chief Light Tech	R. West	7:30a	8:42p	1	Driver	D. Wood	700a	930p		Insert Car			
1	Asst Light Tech	S. Cohagen	7:30a	8:42p	1	Driver	P. Moran	730a	930p		Generator			
1	Elect.	Gittens	7:30a	8:42p	1	Driver	J. Drucker	600a	600p		Crane(s) Stage w/driver			
1	Elect.	Gonzales	7:30a	8:42p	1	Driver	B. Delont	600a	600p		Condor(s)			
1	Elect.	Bonet	7:30a	8:42p	1	Driver	F. Ingram	600a	630p		Scissor Lift(s)			
2	Elect.	Erikson/Neal	7:30a	8:42p		Driver				1	Other: Recreation Trailer			
WARDROBE						Driver					Fuel Truck			
1	Costume Dsgnr.	D. Scott	O/C	O/C		Driver				1	Cast Cars			
1	Costume Supv.	M. Grimaud	O/C	O/C		Driver								
	Asst Cost Dsgnr					Driver								
	Key Costumer					Driver								
1	Set Cost.	Martin	7:30a	9:00p		Driver								
1	Costumer	Zielonka	7:30a	9:00p	10	Total Drivers		10						
	Costumer					Wrangler(s)								
	Costumer					Anml Trnr w/rats								

NOTES & EXPLANATIONS OF DELAYS, ABSENCES, ILLNESSES, SAFETY MTG., ETC.

**Revised finish date due to oneline schedule issued 1/24/95.

* Please note: 82 Bluescreen days to be accounted for on separate report.

FORM NO. FF 605 back (Rev. 4/94)

Director Frank Oz works with the computer-controlled camera.

Director Frank Oz demonstrates the movements of a miniature plastic figure.

An Accurate Portrayal of Native Americans

In the past, movies have not always portrayed Native American tribes accurately. The producers of *The Indian in the Cupboard* wanted to make sure they did not make the same mistake.

Before beginning to film the movie, they invited Chief Lyons of the Onondaga Nation to California to help advise them. The producers learned that there were six different nations in the Iroquois Confederacy, of which Little Bear's nation, the Onondaga, is one.

They were determined to make sure that everything about Little Bear was authentic, including his hair, his costume, his markings, and his tattoos.

The producers hired Jeanne Shenandoah, a member of the Onondaga Nation near Syracuse, New York, to advise them on tribal rituals, ceremonies, clothing, language, and music. She also found Onondagan craftspeople to provide authentic silverwork and beading. Ms. Shenandoah is the daughter of a clan mother and the niece of the head chief of all six nations of the Iroquois Confederacy.

Litefoot learned proper Onondaga tribal dancing and music for his role as Little Bear. Even though Litefoot is Native American, he is a member of the Cherokee Nation, and the Cherokee and Onondaga cultures and rituals are different.

With such attention to detail, you can be sure that what you saw on the screen was accurate!

Hal Scardino as Omri

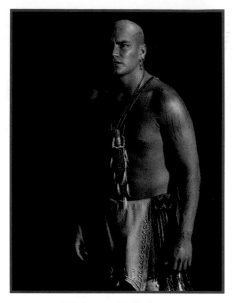

Litefoot as Little Bear

David Keith as Boone

Rishi Bhat as Patrick

The Indian in the Cupboard teaches us that all people have value and that we can all learn from one another. Everyone involved in the making of the movie was proud to be a part of the production.

But now that the movie is over, what will happen to Omri, Patrick, Little Bear, and Boone?

Will they ever meet again?

Is there a sequel in your future?

Stay tuned....